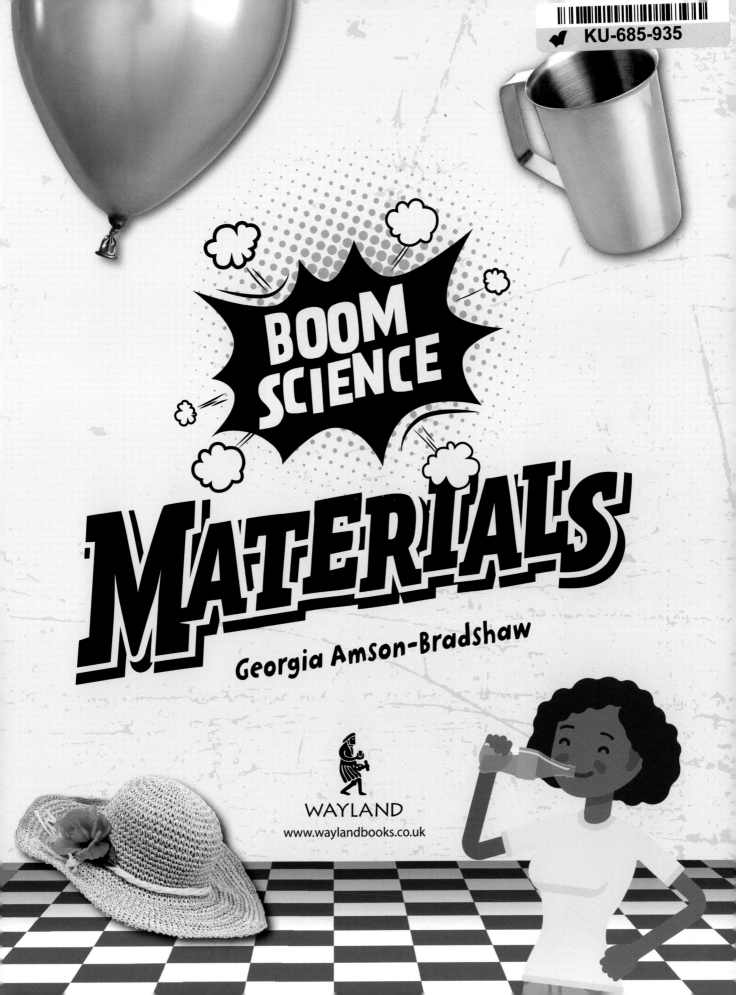

BOOM SCIENCE

MATERIALS

Georgia Amson-Bradshaw

WAYLAND
www.waylandbooks.co.uk

Published in paperback in Great Britain in 2019 by Wayland

Copyright © Hodder and Stoughton Limited, 2018

Produced for Wayland by
White-Thomson Publishing Ltd
www.wtpub.co.uk

Series Editor: Georgia Amson-Bradshaw
Series Designer: Rocket Design (East Anglia) Ltd

ISBN: 978 1 5263 0647 0
10 9 8 7 6 5 4 3 2 1

Wayland
An imprint of
Hachette Children's Group
Part of Hodder & Stoughton
Carmelite House
50 Victoria Embankment
London EC4Y 0DZ

An Hachette UK Company
www.hachette.co.uk
www.hachettechildrens.co.uk

Printed in China

Picture acknowledgements:

Shutterstock: Matyas Rehak 6b, Andrew Rybalko 7t, Dmitrii Kazitsyn 9tl, genjok 9tc, John Kasawa 9tr, Susan Schmitz 10c, cynoclub 10bl, windu 11br, Andrew Rybalko 11t, 11tr, prapann 14t, Okssi 14bl, africanstuff 15t, Teguh Mujiono 15c, Eric Isselee 15b, Nuttapong 17tr, helena0105 17b, Perry Kay 20t, dymax 20c, Anneka 20b, Evgeny Karandaev 21b, senee sriyota 22, vovan 23t, Hayati Kayhan 24, Roman Medvid 25t

Illustrations by Steve Evans 12, 13, 18, 19, 26, 27

All design elements from Shutterstock.

Glossary words are shown in bold.

CONTENTS

MATERIALS

We make things from materials.

PAPER, COTTON, PLASTIC

There are many kinds of **materials**.
This book is made of **paper**. Your clothes
might be made of **cotton** or **plastic**.

WOW!

In Uyuni in Bolivia, some buildings are
made of salt! There is so much salt
in Uyuni that blocks of it can be cut
from the ground and used as bricks.

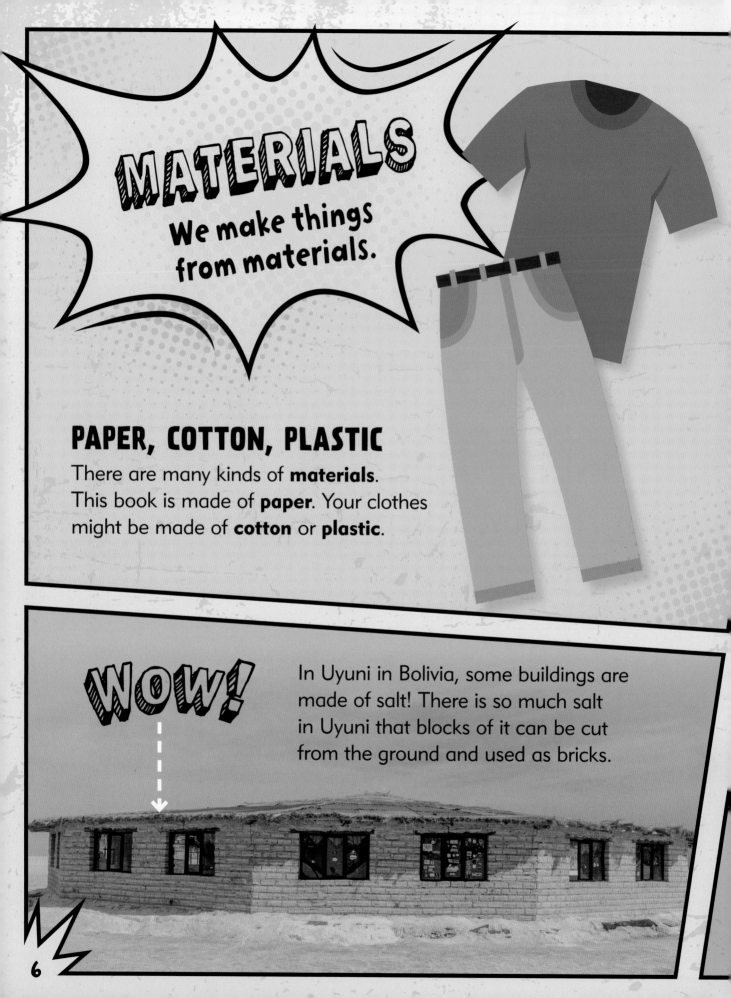

HOW MANY MATERIALS?

Objects can be made of lots of materials, or just one. A drinking glass is just made of one material: **glass**. A computer is made from many materials, including **metal** and plastic.

Oh no! I asked for A glass, not SOME glass!

HEY, WHAT AM I?

Look at these objects. Can you say both the names of the objects, AND the materials the objects are made of?

Object 1

Object 2

Object 3

USING MATERIALS

Some materials have many uses.

MULTI-PURPOSE

Some materials are very useful, because they can do lots of different jobs.

In this picture, the shed and the garden furniture are made of **wood**. The shed's windows and the bottle of fizzy drink are made of glass. The watering can is made of metal, and so is the barbecue.

OPTIONS FOR OBJECTS

The same object can be made of different materials, too. For example, drinking cups can be made from plastic, **ceramic** or metal.

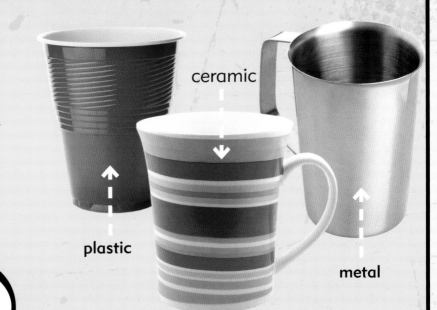

ceramic

plastic

metal

HIDE AND SEEK

Can you spot something people wear on their feet that is made of **waterproof** rubber?

PROPERTIES
A material can be described by its properties.

HARD, SOFT, ROUGH, SMOOTH

Different materials have different **properties**. Properties describe what a material is like. For example, strong or weak, heavy or light, **flexible** or **brittle**.

Oops!

The fabric is soft. It is nice to touch.

Ceramic is brittle. It breaks if you drop it.

UP TO THE JOB

When making objects we use materials that have the best properties for the job. A house needs to be built from strong, **rigid** and waterproof materials. Our clothes need to be made from soft, flexible materials.

This wooden t-shirt isn't very comfy...

My chocolate teapot has melted!

HIDE AND SEEK

A nail is a small object made of hard metal. Can you spot one hiding?

HEY, WHAT AM I?

Can you recognise this rough, hard material? Answer on page 28.

YOUR TURN!

WATERPROOF MATERIALS

Find out which materials let water pass through, and which don't. You'll need:

A plastic or metal tray

Four elastic bands

Four plastic cups

A 15 cm square of foil
A sheet of kitchen roll
A 15 cm square of cling film
A 15 cm square of cloth

A measuring jug of water

STEP ONE

Cover the tops of the cups with the materials. Secure the materials in place with an elastic band around the rims. Make sure there are no gaps around the edges.

STEP TWO

Place the cups onto the tray. Slowly pour 100ml of water onto the top of each covered cup. Make sure you pour the same amount of water onto each.

STEP THREE

Watch what happens to the water. Does it run off or soak through? Remove the elastic bands and the materials and look inside the cups. Which materials let the water through?

The materials that don't let water through are waterproof.

NATURAL MATERIALS

Some materials come from plants, animals or the ground.

This hat started life growing in a field.

MATERIALS THAT GROW

A lot of the materials we use come from plants. Wood comes from trees. Straw is dried stalks of grass and it can be woven to make hats, or used as a building material.

This **wool** jumper is very cosy!

WARM WOOL, SMOOTH SILK

Animals provide us with materials too. Sheep have woolly coats that we shear and use to make woollen jumpers and blankets. Silk comes from the **cocoons** of a type of moth.

STONES AND GEMS

The ground is another place natural materials come from. Stone used in buildings, and precious gems and metals, are found in the ground.

Stones can be polished to make jewellery.

Spiderweb is a super-strong natural material. It is stronger than **steel** is at the same thickness.

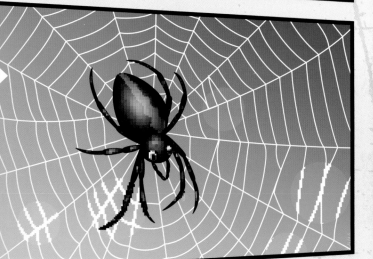

HEY, WHAT AM I?

Which natural material is this?
Answer on page 29.

MAN-MADE MATERIALS

Some materials are made by people.

PLASTIC, PAPER, GLASS

Many everyday materials are created by humans. Common man-made materials, such as plastic, paper and glass, have properties that make them very useful.

plastic computer case

glass computer screen

paper book

plastic bottle

plastic shoes

RAW MATERIAL

The material used to make a new type of material is called the 'raw material'. Paper is usually made from wood, so wood is the raw material for paper. Plastic is made from oil, so oil is the raw material for plastic.

raw material

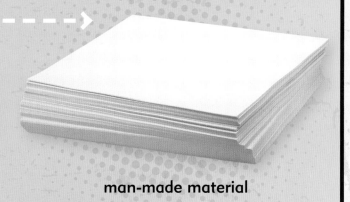

man-made material

STEELY STRONG

Metals such as iron and gold are found naturally in the ground. But some metals, such as steel, are specially made by humans to be extra strong. Man-made metals are mixtures of different types of metal from the ground, and other substances.

HEY, WHAT AM I?

Which common plastic object is this? Answer on page 29.

SORTING MATERIALS

Compare and group materials with these three activities. You'll need:

Around 15 to 20 objects found in your house or garden, such as toys, kitchen items, stones or twigs.

STEP ONE

Sort your assembled objects into two piles. In one pile, put all the objects made entirely or mostly of natural materials. In the other, put all the objects made entirely or mostly of man-made materials.

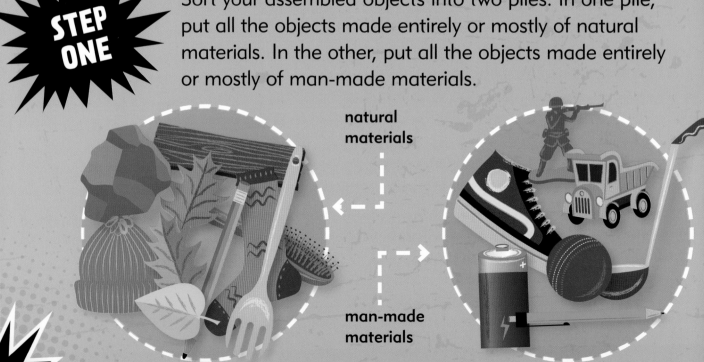

natural materials

man-made materials

STEP TWO

Now sort your objects into new piles based on their properties. Make a pile of rigid objects and flexible objects. Next make a pile of rough objects and smooth objects. What other properties can you divide the objects up by?

rigid objects

flexible objects

STEP THREE

Play this game with a friend. Think of an object. Ask your friend to guess which object you are thinking of by asking questions about its properties, for example, is it shiny or dull? Is it soft or hard? Take turns thinking of objects and guessing.

SOLIDS
Solid materials keep their shape.

SOLID SHAPE

Moving a **solid** object from one container to another doesn't change its shape. If you move a solid apple from a bowl to a plate, the apple stays the same shape.

BEND, TWIST, SQUASH

To change the shape of a solid, we have to reshape it ourselves. Some solid materials can be bent, twisted or squashed.

SWEET SCIENCE

A piece of bubble gum is solid, so it doesn't change shape by itself. But you can change its shape with your hands, or with your mouth!

Spit out that bubble gum!

But Sir, I'm doing science!

The heaviest natural solid is the metal osmium. A tennis ball-sized piece weighs more than eight cans of fizzy drink!

LIQUIDS AND GASES

Liquids can be poured. Gases fill their whole container.

SHAPE SHIFTERS

Materials can be **liquids** or **gases**, as well as solids. Water is a type of liquid material. Air is a type of gas. Unlike solids, liquids and gases do not keep a fixed shape.

POURING DOWN

Liquids can be poured. They always settle at the bottom of their container. This water is changing shape as it is poured into the glass. The water sits at the bottom of the glass.

SPREADING OUT

Gases also change shape, but unlike liquids, they don't settle at the bottom of their container. They spread out to fill it right up. The air inside a balloon fills up the whole balloon.

HEY, WHAT AM I?
Which sweet, fizzy liquid with bubbles of gas in it is this?
Answer on page 29.

HIDE AND SEEK
Milk is a white liquid. Can you spot a puddle of milk spilt somewhere?

HEATING AND COOLING

Heating and cooling materials can change them.

FREEZING AND MELTING

Liquid materials turn to solids if they are cooled down. They turn back into liquids if they are heated up. Think of an ice lolly. It **melts** if you leave it in the sun, but **freezes** hard again if you put it back in the freezer.

I'm melting!

Phew, it's boiling in here!

LIQUIDS AND GASES

Liquids that are heated turn to gases. Gases that are cooled turn back to liquids. Think of water **boiling** in a kettle. Bubbles appear as the liquid water turns into a gas. Steam from a hot shower turns back into water droplets when it touches a mirror's cold surface.

You've really changed.

BURNING

Not all solids melt into liquids. Some solid materials **burn** instead. Think of a wooden match. Unlike ice that has melted, when a match is burnt, it cannot be changed back. It is changed forever.

FREEZING LIQUIDS

Find out which liquids freeze first. You'll need:

A freezer

An ice cube tray

A selection of different liquids such as water, milk, washing-up liquid, oil, vinegar or juice

STEP ONE

Pour a little bit of each liquid into a different section of the ice cube tray. Fill each section two-thirds full. Put the filled ice cube tray into the freezer, and note the time.

What do you think will happen to the liquids?

STEP TWO

Leave the liquids in the freezer for about an hour, then check the tray. Have any of the liquids started to freeze yet? Put the tray back in the freezer.

STEP THREE

Check the liquids roughly every half an hour. Which liquids freeze first? Do any of the liquids not freeze at all?

Why do you think the liquids took different times to freeze? Answer on page 29!

ANSWERS

What am I?

1 I'm a metal fork.
2 I'm a paper newspaper.
3 I'm a plastic bottle.

Hide and Seek Rubber
Wellington boots

Hide and Seek A metal nail

What am I?
I'm a brick.

Page 15

What am I? I'm wool from a sheep.

Page 17

What am I? I'm a plastic bag.

Page 23

What am I? I'm a glass of cola.

Page 23

Hide and Seek Puddle of milk

Page 27 **Your turn**

Liquids freeze at different temperatures. All the liquids in the freezer get colder and colder the longer they are in there. Some liquids only need to cool down a bit before they freeze, so they freeze fast. Other liquids need to cool down a lot more before they freeze, so they take longer to turn solid. Some liquids, such as cooking oil, freeze at very low temperatures: lower than a normal household freezer can go.

GLOSSARY

boil when a liquid heats up and becomes a gas

brittle a material that breaks if you drop it or try to bend it

burn when a material heats up and is changed forever

ceramic a hard material made by baking clay in a hot oven

cocoon a hard case that a caterpillar makes around itself to protect itself while it changes into a moth

cotton a fabric made from fluff that grows on cotton plants

flexible bendy

freeze when a liquid cools down and becomes solid

gas a material with no fixed shape that spreads out to fill its whole container

glass a hard, man-made material that you can see through

liquid a material with no fixed shape that can be poured

material the stuff that an object is made from is called a material

melt when a solid is heated up and becomes liquid

metal a material that is normally hard and shiny

paper a man-made material made from wood

plastic a hard, man-made material that can be moulded into any shape

property a way of describing a material, such as hard or soft

rigid not bendy

solid a material that keeps a fixed shape

steel a type of man-made metal, made by mixing naturally occurring metals together

waterproof a material that does not let water pass through

wood a natural material that we take from trees

wool a natural material made from a sheep's coat

INDEX

Boom Science Series contents lists

ELECTRICITY

- ★ ELECTRICITY AND ENERGY
- ★ USING ELECTRICITY
- ★ YOUR TURN: Electricity hunt
- ★ NATURAL ELECTRICITY
- ★ BATTERIES
- ★ CIRCUITS
- ★ YOUR TURN: Make a battery
- ★ SWITCHES
- ★ MAKING ELECTRICITY
- ★ STAYING SAFE
- ★ YOUR TURN: Make a switch

FORCES

- ★ PUSHES AND PULLS
- ★ GRAVITY
- ★ WEIGHT
- ★ YOUR TURN: Forces at the playground
- ★ FRICTION
- ★ WATER RESISTANCE
- ★ AIR RESISTANCE
- ★ YOUR TURN: Make a parachute
- ★ MAGNETS
- ★ SIMPLE MACHINES
- ★ YOUR TURN: Make simple machines

HUMAN BODY

- ★ HEALTHY BODY
- ★ SKELETON AND BONES
- ★ MUSCLES
- ★ YOUR TURN: Make a model arm
- ★ DIGESTIVE SYSTEM
- ★ HEART AND BLOOD
- ★ BREATHING
- ★ YOUR TURN: How big are your lungs?
- ★ BRAIN AND NERVES
- ★ SENSES
- ★ YOUR TURN: Test your senses

LIGHT

- ★ LIGHT
- ★ NATURAL AND MAN-MADE LIGHT
- ★ LIGHT AND MATERIALS
- ★ YOUR TURN: Paint pictures with light
- ★ SHADOWS
- ★ SEEING
- ★ MIRRORS
- ★ YOUR TURN: Make shadow puppets
- ★ COLOUR
- ★ LIVING THINGS
- ★ YOUR TURN: Make a colour spinner

MATERIALS

- ★ MATERIALS
- ★ USING MATERIALS
- ★ PROPERTIES
- ★ YOUR TURN: Waterproof materials
- ★ NATURAL MATERIALS
- ★ MAN-MADE MATERIALS
- ★ YOUR TURN: Sorting materials
- ★ SOLIDS
- ★ LIQUIDS AND GASES
- ★ HEATING AND COOLING MATERIALS
- ★ YOUR TURN: Freezing materials

PLANTS

- ★ PLANTS
- ★ ROOTS AND STEMS
- ★ YOUR TURN: Colour change celery
- ★ LEAVES
- ★ FLOWERS
- ★ FRUIT
- ★ SEEDS AND BULBS
- ★ YOUR TURN: Grow a bulb in water
- ★ SUNLIGHT
- ★ WATER AND WARMTH
- ★ YOUR TURN: Plant maze

SEASONS

- ★ FOUR SEASONS
- ★ SPRING
- ★ SUMMER
- ★ YOUR TURN: Make a rain gauge
- ★ AUTUMN
- ★ WINTER
- ★ YOUR TURN: Make frost
- ★ ANIMALS
- ★ PLANTS
- ★ CELEBRATIONS
- ★ YOUR TURN: Build a bug hotel

SOUND

- ★ SOUND WAVES
- ★ HEARING
- ★ YOUR TURN: Improve your ears
- ★ MAKING SOUNDS
- ★ LOUD AND SOFT
- ★ HIGH AND LOW
- ★ YOUR TURN: Guess the sound
- ★ ECHOES
- ★ MUSIC
- ★ ANIMAL SOUNDS
- ★ YOUR TURN: Make music